The Dancing Salmon

An Alaskan Folklore Tale of the Northern Lights
Written By: The Lone Alaskan Gypsy
Illustrated By: David Dodson

DEDICATION

This book is dedicated to the funny, smart, beautiful, and absolutely wonderful children of the Yukon River delta in Alaska. The children who inspired this book. The children who reside in Mountain Village, Kotlik, Alakanuk, Emmonak, Nunam Iqua, Scammon Bay, Hooper Bay, Chevak, St. Mary's, Pitka's Point, Pilot Station, Marshall, and Russian Mission. You are all the most delightful kids I have had the pleasure of meeting, and I love each and every one of you with all of my heart. Know that the magic in this book was inspired by the magic in your lives. Each of you have the most lovely of stories to tell- all you need to do is start writing.

"Goodnight, sleep tight, dream dreams that take you on great explorations in the moonlight," said Ihana's mom as she switched off her bedroom light. Ihana laid down and rested her head on her pillow. The room turned from sunlight to shadows in an instant. She stared at the ceiling for a while as her eyes grew accustomed to the lack of brightness. Soon enough the shadows didn't seem so dark anymore, in fact they seemed rather light. She turned her head to look out her window, curious if a bright moon was the reason for the night-light aura, but as she peered out her tiny bedroom window, her eyes caught a different sight. A bright green streak of northern lights lit up the entire star-spotted landscape.

Ihana was so excited- for she dearly loved northern lights. She jumped down from her bed and tiptoed through the hallway and across the kitchen until she reached her front door. She slowly twisted the knob and then stepped out into the frigid cold winter air. It nipped at her cheeks and nose. She shivered for a second and then quickly ran inside to grab her boots, parka, and fur mittens. Once she was dressed appropriately she again stepped into the night. The snow glowed sparkling green, reflecting the dancing lights above. Her eyes followed the twinkle of the fallen flakes. And then she peered up into the sky. To the north side of her home stood a large array of giant spruce trees. It was a thick forest, and one that blocked her view of the northern lights. The lights danced above her, but they also danced just beyond the tip of the trees. And she could only see those particular lights when they jumped above the tree tops. She wondered quite deeply what those lights looked like. Were they dancing to the same tune as the ones directly above her house?

She tried very hard to peer over the trees, but even from her tip-toes she couldn't manage to get a full view of the aurora above. She sat for a moment, frustrated with the timber. Then she decided that she would walk through the forest, to the other side, so she could see the lights in all their glory.

And so she trekked, into the trees, into the shadows. Once under the cover of the evergreen branches, Ihana's world was no longer bright. In fact it was very dark. So dark that she had to strain her eyes to see beyond her next footstep. At first Ihana was scared- for she never really cared for pure black darkness. But after a while her eyes adjusted and she got comfortable with the rhythm of her forest walk. It was early winter, so there was only a very thin layer of snow on the ground, which made walking quite easy.

She walked for quite some time. She passed two weasels fighting over a carcass in the snow. And a little later she crossed paths with a red fox prancing around hunting for mice. She even met a little boreal owl- and he hooted in her presence. But eventually she finally made her way to the other side of the forest. She had crossed many hills, and even a mountain, and her legs were oh so tired. But the sight before her was one to behold. The land was flat tundra, covered completely in white snow and dotted with the rare willow or alder bush. And the lights, they were there. Brighter than she had ever seen lights before. They were dancing quickly and vibrantly and actively. They were energetic and fun and everywhere. They shot out in every direction! They twinkled to the north and gleamed to the west. In the east they sparkled and in the south they frolicked.

Ihana's eyes lit up. It was magical and a large smile grew on her face. She sat down in the snow to rest her tired feet. She let her eyes wander into the movement of the green glimmer in the stars. She sat for a very very long time. Her eyes traced every single angle of the aurora. As she reached the most northern lights she began to trace them as well, but then something surprised her. As she followed the green shimmer down and down she saw a spot where it touched the ground. At that spot the lights were brighter than any other part of the sky.

Ihana's curiosity grew as her eyes stayed on the place where the glitter met the ground. She debated for a while whether or not to walk to that particular spot. But eventually she made up her mind, and her feet began walking forward. The land ahead of her was pure white snow. It was flat, and hard. The tundra in the summer is soft and bumpy (which makes for difficult walking). But with the few inches of snow that winter had already brought, the ground had become just as comfortable as a city sidewalk.

She walked for many many miles across the land. Her eyes never once veered from the place where the northern lights shined the brightest. It took her many hours to walk as far as she did and when she got closer she noticed that the lights ended on the very top of a low rolling hill. It was the only hill within sight. From horizon to horizon in any direction the world was flat. But right before her, stood a small hill and atop it the most magical glowing scene.

She began to get excited and walked faster to reach the spot. As she reached the base of the hill she looked up and noticed a small shadowy object. She peered as hard as she could to see through the darkness, but couldn't quite make out what it was. She started to run forward, for she really really wanted to know what the shadow was. When she had ran halfway up the hill she finally could make out what the shadow was. It was a very small cabin, made of old scraggly logs. It was haphazardly put together and very worn from the harsh arctic winds.

The lights were very very bright now. They sparkled like a waterfall of glitter and she didn't feel so tired anymore. She had a renewed energy and finally climbed up the last bit of the way to make it to the very spot where the northern lights touched the ground. As she reached the top of the hill, her pace slowed immensely. The view caught her off guard and she was in awe.

Where the green sparkles hit the ground sat a beautiful pool of crystal clear water. As the lights entered the water they lit it up and within you could see beautiful bright fish swimming slowly and elegantly around the pond. Tucked away in the shadows right next to the pond, sat the little cabin. It looked warming, kind, and not so worn when it was in the light of the aurora. Ihana walked over very slowly, carefully, as if not to alter one aspect of the beautiful scene. When she reached the side of the pond, she knelt down and peered inside. Below her was a never ending array of beautiful salmon swimming softly and peacefully in the bright water. They almost seemed to slow dance as they swayed their back tails to and fro through the water.

Her eyes followed the small twinkles in the pond. They looked like stars, glimmering in and out as they rose from the water and into the air. She followed them from the warmth of pool to chilling arctic landscape. They went into the air- magically. They had a bit of a see-through appearance. She could barely see beyond the other side. But within them there were millions of tiny fairy-like glitters floating up and up into the sky. Around them swirled a bright vibrant green haze. It was fog-like but gorgeous. Not the heavy fog that blocks a morning from awaking, but rather an inspiring sunrise fog that brings forth an entirely new perspective on what daylight means.

She was caught up in the light and didn't notice when behind her the door to the cabin squeaked open and old man stepped out into the world. He used a diamond willow wooden cane to keep his balance as he slowly maneuvered down his stairs and across his front yard, to the side of his house where the pond sat.

She didn't see him until he was a few feet away. She was startled when she caught sight of the shadow of his figure out of the corner of her eye. She jumped a little and then rose in his presence. He was a very old looking man. He had tan skin and tired eyes. His hair was gray. He had a medium-length scruffy beard. He was short, but also a bit hunched over- so his poor posture made him appear a few inches lower than he had stood at a younger age.

Ihana didn't know what to say, so she stood silent for a while. Finally she stuttered, "Wh-What's your name?"

The man looked her right in the eye. His eyes were a warm brown, and once she saw the kindness in his stare, she was no longer nervous. "Flynt," answered the man. "And yours?" he asked.

"Ihana," she answered smiling.

"What brings you here, Ihana?" asked the man.

"I just wanted to see where the northern lights touched the ground," explained Ihana.

The man nodded. "And so you found it," he said.

Ihana nodded, and smiled at the lights to the side of her.

"Would you like to come in and warm up before you go home?" asked Flynt.

Ihana nodded. And so Flynt turned around and slowly trudged inside. Ihana followed behind him and glanced back at the northern lights as they turned around the corner of the cabin that lead to the front door. Flynt stumbled up the stairs and pushed open the plywood door. Ihana followed him cautiously into his home.

Inside was a small wood stove, a wooden table, and a kitchen sink in the corner. It was a dark shadowy home, but the large window to the side of the door let in enough light from the northern lights that it lit up the entire room. Flynt shuffled over to the table and sat down. He then offered Ihana a seat. Ihana sat. In the dim light of the northern lights she could barely make out the figure of the old man sitting across from her. But even in the darkness she could see he was very thin. He almost looked starved. He had wide cheeks, but they were skeleton looking. His hands were merely skin and bone.

Then Ihana asked, "Why do you live here?"

Flynt smiled. "I care for the salmon," he said.

"What do you eat?" she asked.

Flynt sighed, and paused for a second. "Not very much," he answered, "Blackfish that I catch in my trap, some rabbits and ptarmigan that I can hunt on days when I am able."

"But... you look so hungry," answered Ihana. "Why don't you just eat the salmon?" she asked, looking out the window to the lights.

"Oh no, I can't eat the salmon," said Flynt, "they supply the northern lights."

"But you could just eat one, to cure your hunger," Ihana said.

"One fish, supplies one line of northern lights. Who knows where that line would have lead or what joy it would have brought to the world." He sighed... looking out with a tired smile to the lights beyond his window.

"But you're so hungry..." muttered Ihana, "It's only one fish..."

Flynt looked at her and smiled. "Come with me young child," he said and began to get up. He struggled for a second to leave his chair, but once he was standing he quickly shuffled to the door and then outside into his yard. Ihana followed closely, until he reached the pond. He stood beside the water for an instant looking down. Ihana came and stood beside him to see what he was peering into. As she looked down she felt his hand touch her back, and then with one swift push he knocked her feet from the edge and she fell into the water.

Ihana panicked and immediately began flailing her arms trying to rise to the surface. She held her breath and opened her eyes in the hopes of finding air again. But as she opened her eyes something happened. A tangle of her hair floated out in front of her in the water, but everything else looked beautiful. All of the sudden she didn't feel as if she needed to hold her breath and she inhaled deeply. Air, not water, filled her lungs. Her heartbeat slowed to a normal level and her scared shaking subsided. Salmon were swimming around her in the green glowing water. They were beautiful, happy, but they didn't seem to notice her presence. She twirled in the water to get a full view of the pond. The glowing fish were shiny shades of blue, gold, purple, and green.

Suddenly one of the salmon swam right beside her. It wrapped her arms around its body and then dove from the water and up into the sky. Ihana held on tightly as the fish swam up into the northern lights above. It went high into the sky and continued swimming along the edge of a bright green light. It swam for many minutes. And then, in an instant, it jumped from the green stream and down to the landscape. It free-fell, leaving a stream of sparkling green behind it. It dove right next to the back porch of a little cabin tucked away on the side of a mountain.

Ihana closed her eyes when she saw the ground getting closer. She reached out to brace herself for the fall, but she never landed. All of the sudden her feet were tucked nicely into the snow and everything was fine. She opened her eyes and peered around the corner of the porch of the cabin she had landed beside. On the porch sat a very old couple. They were on a swing, in the dark, holding hands.

"Oh, it's been so many years we've watched this show- but this must be one of the most beautiful I've seen," said the old woman in a very tired shaky voice.

"Yes," mumbled the old man, "it's very beautiful." There was a long pause and then the old man turned to his wife. He grabbed her hand and said in a very quiet whisper, "but not as beautiful as you."

The woman smiled the biggest grin. Her tired eyes lightened just a little. "Oh, you old man," she laughed, "compliments never grow old with you do they?"

He laughed with her, and softly kissed her forehead. She rested her little bit of hair on his shoulder and the both of them snuggled in to finish watching the show. Their eyes filled with intrigue as they watched an image even their aged knowledge couldn't fathom. As Ihana looked up to the sky, before she could see the lights, the fish swooped down again and caught her on its back. It swam up and up and rejoined the river of sparkling green.

Ihana looked out over her shoulder. The stars seemed almost in reach. And the glitter of the aurora enlightened her soul just as vibrantly as it changed the hues of the sky. She didn't know, but the night she was experiencing would change her forever. The second time the salmon jumped from the sky, Ihana was still startled. But this time she wasn't as afraid. As she neared the ground- once again she closed her eyes. When she felt her feet flattened against the ground she opened them.

This time she was hidden deep in a willow timber. The trees were short, but thick. There was an opening not far from her. And the young girl in the clearing looked as young as she was. The girl looked up to the sky. She was standing there, looking very small amidst the landscape. She had a tiny fur coat and snow pants on. Her hands were covered in purple knit mittens- that matched her scarf and hat. Her eyes weren't as intrigued as the elderly couple's. Instead... hers were hopeful. Hopeful with the slightest tinge of sad.

"Mom," she said- in a voice that cracked with a crying sob. A tiny tear fell down from her eye. She tried to talk again, but her voice got scratchy in the cold. The lump in her throat didn't help. "Mom," she began again- this time in a quieter voice. "Dad said if I talked to the northern lights they'd take my message to you. So I wanted to show you that I'm wearing the gloves you made me." She looked down at her gloves and smiled a little. "And the scarf." She picked up her scarf and lightly nuzzled the soft material with her cheek. "And the hat!" she was a bit more excited this time as she remembered the hat as well. She pressed her mittens to it- showing the stars the lovely trinket her mother had made her.

"I had lots of fun at school yesterday. My teacher let us make cookies. Except they weren't cookies that you put in the oven like we make. These were 'no bake' cookies." Explained the little girl. The choke in her throat seemed to disappear as she continued talking. She went on and on, telling her mother all sorts of things. About her brothers (and how much they annoyed her) and about her best friend and the boy she thought was cute and about how she wanted to paint her room blue because pink was for little kids. She went on for the longest time and Ihana listened to it all. The lights would nod when the little girl spoke to them. They would laugh when she told a joke and move surprisingly fast if she told an exciting story. They listened to her intently- just like her mother's ear. Perhaps they were her mother's ear.

But before the little girl finished and before Ihana would know whether or not her mother was listening- the salmon picked her up again. And off she went- riding into the lighted darkness. She rode for a very long time this time. She passed over mountains and lakes and forests and tundra. The wind brushed her cheeks and lightly flicked her hair. And just as she reached a mountain with a tiny trail leading up the side, she landed.

When she opened her eyes this time, no one was there. But there was a small wobbly road, and so she followed it. There were foot prints and she followed them. As she did so, she began to hear the soft prance of footsteps not far ahead. She ran to catch up to them. When she got to them she spotted a young woman with a large backpack. She was huffing and puffing- muttering under her breath about how she would never take a long hike in the dark again. She walked for quite some ways before she reached a clearing in the trees. She peered over a large cliff and then looked up to the sky. She gasped a little when she saw the bright green streaks above her. At that moment every doubt she had had about her decision to trek in the dark disappeared. She sat in awe for what seemed like fifteen minutes. Completely silent. Unwavering. Her absence of noise was broken with the stomping boots of a young man trekking down the trail.

When he reached the opening he was surprised by her appearance. He jumped a bit- snapping out of his mindless walking thoughts. "Oh hi..." he stuttered.

"Hi..." she whispered back, as to not break the silence with the harshness of a loud voice.

"What are you doing walking so late?" he asked.

"I honestly have no idea. Thought it would be exciting. I was beginning to doubt myself until I saw this," she said- pointing up to the opening in the trees. The man walked over far enough to see the sky without the blockage of the spruce branches.

"Wow..." he whispered in a speechless voice.

"I know..." she said back, smirking slightly at his amazement.

"I've been walking all night in the shadows. I didn't even notice," he laughed.

"Me neither, until I got too lazy to walk," laughed the girl back to him.

"They always say life is about moving and going forward and working towards something," the boy said, "Hikes are kind of like that. We do a lot of going somewhere. But sometimes it's pretty amazing what you can see if you just stop looking for something better and notice what's already right in front of you."

The girl looked at him, surprised by his philosophical words. "It is pretty amazing. It's also amazing how the only two people in an entire national park can end up trekking the same trail on the same night and stop at the same spot to see the same northern lights."

The guy laughed, a really loud real laugh that stirred up the night. And the girl laughed too, a quirky laugh- but a beautiful one. And they spent hours talking... just talking as the lights played above them.

Ihana didn't get to hear their entire conversation. As their laughs billowed into the night the salmon picked her up for the last time. And this time the salmon swam the opposite direction and swished its tail softly home. When it got to the pond that it had originated from it left Ihana on the side, near the old man who lived in the cabin, and then swam away into the sky. It left the river of green, and went out with a small streak of red following behind it.

"Why is it red?" Ihana asked, noticing the pinkish hue as it swam into the darkness.

"It's dieing," said the man.

"But why?" Ihana asked sadly.

"Because, my dear child, it's had its life. It lived in the pond and it flew the skies. It saw beautiful things and made the river glow. And it brightened lives- just as it was meant to. Do you remember the old couple you saw?" he asked.

Ihana nodded.

"Tomorrow morning the old lady will pass away. But the old man will not be sad. It was her time. And he had the miracle of spending her last night admiring a show they have watched since the day they met. Remember that couple on the mountain?"

"That was them?" Ihana asked, surprised.

"Oh no," laughed the old man, "But it's the a couple just like them. Tonight the northern lights brought soul mates together. That doesn't happen with just any night, Ihana. Stars align and the lights glow bright only for very very special nights."

"What about the girl my age? What happened to her?"

"Her mother heard every word she said. She sat right on the edge of the northern lights and laughed and cried and excitedly replied to every word her daughter spoke. And she will for the next sixty years her daughter speaks to the lights. She'll always be there, on the side of the special aurora she sends her daughter some nights."

Ihana sat quietly for a while. She looked at the old man as he stood entranced by the pond. He was very very tired looking. Very weak. Very thin... very hungry. But she understood now. "And that's why you can't eat the salmon. Because they need to make the northern lights- they need to make death okay and bring soul mates together and give messages to angels?" asked Ihana.

The man smiled and placed his hand on her shoulder. "You, my child, are very bright. How could I ever eat a salmon that lightens the lives of other people? How could I feed myself and take away the joy of others? I could never do that, Ihana. This pond could make my dinner for a month or it could supply others happiness for a lifetime."

Ihana looked up to the old man with the biggest smile on her face and then, without one more word, she began her trek home- to her bedroom, where she could watch the lights and know the salmon from the comfort of her covers. And the old man, with a lesson taught and a happy heart, went to dine on the feast of humility.

Made in the USA
Middletown, DE
04 June 2018